Big Billy's Great Adventure

A Story about the Love of God

Big Billy's Great Adventure

by Sheila Walsh

Illustrations by Jason Lynch

www.tommynelson.com

A Division of Thomas Nelson, Inc.
www.ThomasNelson.com

This book is dedicated with love to my son, Christian.
One of the greatest joys in life is being your mom.

Text & illustrations copyright © 2003 by Sheila Walsh

Illustrated by Jason Lynch; endsheets illustrated by Don Sullivan

Gnoo Zoo characters copyright © 2001 by Aslan Entertainment and Children of Faith. Gnoo Zoo is a trademark of Aslan Entertainment.

Published in Nashville, Tennessee, by Tommy Nelson®, a Division of Thomas Nelson, Inc.

Scripture quoted from the *International Children's Bible®, New Century Version®*, copyright © 1986, 1988, 1999 by Tommy Nelson®, a Division of Thomas Nelson, Inc., Nashville, Tennessee 37214. Used by permission.

Library of Congress Cataloging-in-Publication Data

Walsh, Sheila.
    Big Billy's great adventure / by Sheila Walsh ; illustrations by Jason Lynch.
        p. cm. -- (Gnoo Zoo ; bk. 5)
    Sequel to: Miss Marble's marvelous makeover
    Summary: Still threatened by the evil Reptillion and Creepshaw, Big Billy must leave the other carousel animals and go on part of the great adventure alone, except for the Great White Tiger, who dwells in his heart.
    ISBN 1-4003-0235-8
    [1. Love--Fiction. 2. Conduct of life--Fiction. 3. Merry-go-round--Fiction.] I. Lynch, Jason, ill. II. Title. III. Series.

PZ7.W16894Bi 2003
    [Fic]--dc21

                                                                                    2003003874

Printed in the United States of America

03 04 05 06 LBK 5 4 3 2 1

Dear Parents,

I remember a conversation I had with my son when he was three years old:

"Mommy, what is God like?"

"He is wonderful, darling, and he loves you all the time."

"Even when I'm naughty?" he asked, a world of possibility opening up before his mischievous eyes.

"Even when you are naughty," I confirmed, wondering if I had just given my son a lifelong get-out-of-jail-free card.

But that's the tension of the gospel, the overwhelming reality that we are loved on our good days and on our bad days, not based on our performance but on God's heart. It's a gift. It's a miracle.

Even as I write, I think of the moms and dads, the grandparents who might have forgotten this truth. So often, what starts out as an adventure in faith becomes a labor of performance, where we think that our behavior affects God's heart towards us. That's never true. God's love for us is based on who he is, not on how well we do.

There is no greater joy in life than communicating the unconditional love and grace of God to children, young or old. That's why I wrote this book. I want my son, Christian, to understand that he is loved, always loved by God. I want *you* to know that, too.

In this book, our friends from the Gnoo Zoo, a mythical land representing Earth, continue their adventure to find their way home to the Great White Tiger, our Father God, who made them and loves them. There are obstacles on the way, but the greatest adventure is learning to love and trust God on the journey.

Thank you for inviting us into your hearts and homes. It is a sacred trust.

Let the adventure begin!

Sheila Walsh

"Yes, I am sure that nothing can separate us from the love God has for us. Not death, not life, not angels, not ruling spirits, nothing now, nothing in the future, no powers, nothing above us, nothing below us, or anything else in the whole world will ever be able to separate us from the love of God that is in Christ Jesus our Lord."

—Romans 8:38–39

Big Billy sat at the edge of the Sea of Glass, gazing up at the stars. He thought back to the days when he and his friends had been prisoners on the Gnoo Zoo carousel, held captive by the evil Reptillion. Big Billy had escaped with his friends, but now it was time to return and set the other animals free, too.

"Great White Tiger," Big Billy began, "this has been a great adventure—the greatest adventure of my life, of all of our lives."

He looked at his friends who were asleep, piled up in a heap behind him. There was Einstein, the brilliant but eccentric elephant; Miss Marbles, the prissy but kindhearted ostrich; and Chattaboonga and Boongachatta, the tomboy twin monkeys.

Big Billy looked toward the sky and spoke, "You have protected us through so much danger, but now I'm afraid. How will we ever get across this terrible sea?"

"Trust me, my son. I will provide a way. But you, Big Billy, must first go alone and then return for your friends," the Great White Tiger replied.

"Alone? Oh dear!" Big Billy exclaimed, causing his friends to stir from their sleep. "I trust *you*. I just don't trust *me*. What if I mess up?"

"I will always be there for you," the Great White Tiger replied, "and I will help you find the way."

"That's right!" Chattaboonga cried as she bounced onto Big Billy's shoulders. "Remember how he was there for me when I took the wrong path and was captured by old stinky breath and his pathetic partner?" she asked, referring to the evil Reptillion and his scrawny sidekick Creepshaw.

"And he was there for me, even after my overwhelming love for chocolate caused us all a delay in getting back to the carousel," Einstein added as he ambled over to the water's edge.

"Well, I must also confess," Miss Marbles chirped. "There *was* that time when I ignored the Great White Tiger's helper and ended up with my feathers all awhirl, heading down the river toward the waterfall. He protected me then." She batted her eyelashes. "But my beautiful purse has never been the same."

"Yes, I remember," Big Billy said with a smile.

"And remember this," the Great White Tiger said, "remember that I love you all, and I will always love you." Then he turned to Big Billy. "Now, Billy, it is time to go. The enemy is near, but I am closer; I'm in your heart. To cross the Sea of Glass, you must trust what is in your heart and not what your eyes or ears tell you."

"Ooooh," Reptillion whispered, "this is better than I had hoped for in my wildest, most evil dreams!"

"Yeah, boss!" Creepshaw added. "Piece of cake!"

"If perchance there is a candy store on the other side, a morsel of chocolate would be greatly appreciated," Einstein said.

"Should there be an institution of beauty, perhaps you could book an appointment for me to have my feathers fluffed," Miss Marbles added.

"Have you forgotten what this great adventure is all about?" Big Billy asked. "We must return to the carousel so that our friends can be free, too."

"Right, right, right," they all muttered at once.

"When you get to the other side," the Great White Tiger said, "Raymond the Purple Piranha will provide a boat that will take you back to your friends. You will then all return safely to the carousel."

"Piranha fish! Piranha fish!" Boongachatta screeched, jumping into Einstein's arms. "You'll be fish bait, Billy! A salty snack!"

"Trust me now, Billy, and take your first step," encouraged the Great White Tiger.

Big Billy stepped onto the Sea of Glass. *It seems pretty sturdy*, he thought. *This might not be so hard after all.* He took a few more steps. "I'm doing it! I'm doing it!" he cried.

Just then, a hand reached out of a hole in the sea and grabbed Billy by the leg.

"Help! Help!" Billy cried.

"I've got you this time!" Reptillion growled as he pulled Billy closer and closer to the edge.

"Help me, Great White Tiger!" Billy pleaded as he began to disappear into the sea.

Then, suddenly, from overhead, Big Billy heard, "Tallyho! Toodaloo and company to the rescue!"

Big Billy looked up and saw his old friends Toodaloo and Lulu. The Great White Tiger's helpers circled the hole with a rope.

Lulu called down to Big Billy, "Grab on, ol' buddy!"

Billy reached up and grabbed the rope.

"I say, ol' chap, you seemed to be in a bit of a bother there," Toodaloo said.

"I think I got a little carried away with myself," sighed Big Billy.

"Well, you're safe now, little buddy," Lulu said as she flew off. "The great adventure continues!"

Reptillion shouted from below, "We'll be back! We have more in store for you."

As Billy continued along, he looked at the vast sea ahead of him. "That's my problem," he said to himself. "I'm hopeless! I always get into trouble. I never get it right."

"That's right. You'll never make it across!" Reptillion's voice boomed.

"Yeah, I don't know why the Not-So-Great White Tiger chose you," Creepshaw added. "You're not worth saving!"

Billy sat down, discouraged. Suddenly the sea began to shake. Cracks appeared in the glass, sending splinters flying everywhere. The sea opened like the mouth of a dragon and swallowed Big Billy whole.

Down, down, down, he went spinning out of control. He was too dizzy and too weak to cry out for help. He took one glance at the mark of the Great White Tiger on his paw and closed his eyes.

Just when he thought he was doomed, he felt someone beside him. He opened his eyes and saw a large, blue sea horse with a silver saddle.

"Hop on!" Scooter said.

Billy jumped into the saddle and they took off, up, up, higher and higher, until they were above the sea.

"Well, shiver my scales! What happened to you?" Scooter asked as they landed.

"I don't know," Big Billy said. "I was just sitting there, thinking that I don't deserve the love of the Great White Tiger. The next thing I know, I'm falling into the middle of the sea!"

"That's where you went wrong, my friend. You cannot *earn* the love of the Great White Tiger. It's a gift. You always have it," Scooter said.

"One day," Big Billy wished, "I just want to get it *all* right."

"Big Billy, he loves you every day, good days and bad days," Scooter replied. "Now, there's no time to waste. Off you go." With a flick of his tail, Scooter was gone.

As Big Billy continued on his great adventure, a thick mist began to rise from the sea. It swirled around him in waves, blinding him. Suddenly, the howling of a dozen snow wolves froze Big Billy in his tracks. He felt their hot breath on his legs and heard them snap at his feet.

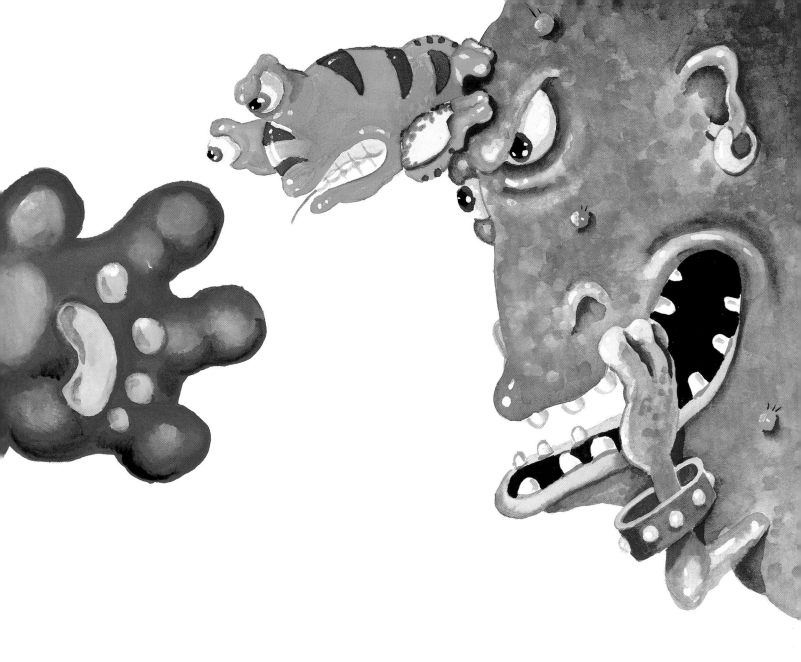

"Great White Tiger," Big Billy whispered, "I am so afraid. But I will trust that you are with me. I believe you love me, no matter what."

He started to walk again, and as he walked, he smiled as the howls just faded into the mist.

"I told you the wolf thing was a lame idea," Creepshaw whispered.

"Silence! What is that foolish bear most afraid of?" Reptillion huffed.

Creepshaw thought a moment. "Losing his dumb friends?" he wondered aloud.

"Brilliant!" Reptillion replied, beginning to devise a plan.

Big Billy could see the shore. He was almost all the way across the Sea of Glass! When he was just steps away from shore, he heard, "Big Billy, help me!"

Billy listened carefully. He heard the cry again. It was coming from behind him.

"Help me, Big Billy! Help me! I am sinking!" It sounded like Miss Marbles!

"Oh! What should I do?!" Big Billy cried out.

"You must come back, Big Billy. I need your help," the voice pleaded.

"Yeah, we, I mean, *I* need your help. It's me, Miss Marbles. Don't you recognize my voice??" another added, with an evil chuckle.

Deep in Billy's heart, he could hear the Great White Tiger's voice: "You must trust what is in your heart and not what your eyes or ears tell you."

Big Billy focused on the shore ahead and kept walking.

"Your voice sounds nothing like Miss Marbles, Your Royal Nastiness," Creepshaw said to Reptillion, watching Big Billy continue.

"Silence, fool! Will nothing get that bear to turn around?" Reptillion demanded.

Billy's feet finally hit the shore. He could feel the sand between his toes and the warmth of the sunlight on his face. The hard, smooth Sea of Glass transformed into rolling waves again.

Just then, a giant fish leapt out of the water.

"Hiya! Hiya! Hiya! I am Raymond. It's an honor to meet you!" The large piranha splashed along the shoreline and led Big Billy to a crystal boat with a large yellow sail. "Climb aboard," he told Big Billy. "After you retrieve your friends from the other shore, this boat will take you all safely home to the Gnoo Zoo carousel."

Big Billy stood on the bow of the boat, and it began to glide through the water, slowly at first, then faster and faster until Billy was breathless in the wind.

"You did it, Billy! You did it!" his friends cried, as he returned to the shore where they waited.

"You mean the Great White Tiger did it!" Billy said, smiling. He hugged each of his friends as they climbed aboard. "What a great adventure!" he shouted. He raised the True Gnoo Key to the sky. "To the carousel!"

"To the carousel!" the rest of the gang cheered.

With that, a tornado of twinkly stars began to whirl around them, gathering speed until it swooshed the boat up in the air and pushed it across the sky like a meteor. When the boat landed again, Big Billy could see they were finally home at the Gnoo Zoo.

"Oh no you don't, Big Billy!" Reptillion whispered. "Not if I can help it!"

"I say, mate, isn't that the old crew?" the toucan asked, watching five familiar figures at the bottom of the hill.

"Well, what do you know! It's Big Billy . . . and . . . Miss Marbles . . . and the whole gang!" the alligator exclaimed. "I never thought we'd see you again!" he called to his friends as they drew closer. "Life has been so hard since you left on your great adventure!"

"Did you find the Great White Tiger?" asked a timid giraffe.

"We sure did!" Big Billy said with a smile, taking the True Gnoo Key out of his pocket.

He raised the key to insert it in the Gnoo Zoo's empty keyhole when, suddenly, Reptillion came roaring out of the trees!

"Give that key to me!" Reptillion demanded.

"Never!" Billy cried, clutching the key to his chest.

Reptillion grabbed Billy by the ankles. "Now you will obey," he hissed.

"We will never serve you," Billy said. "We serve the Great White Tiger. He loves us and we love him." With that, Billy wiggled himself free. He put the True Gnoo Key back in its rightful place with a click.

The carousel began to spin. Lights came on and music filled the air. The spindly poles that once held the animals captive disappeared . . . forever.

"Aaargh! Stop that infernal noise," Reptillion cried. "I'll be back one day. You'll see!"

"Hooray!" the animals cried together. "We're free! Now we will be able to take children on the carousel ride of their lives!"

"And the adventure is just beginning!" the Great White Tiger said with joy.

"What? Just beginning?" Big Billy asked. "I thought this was the *end* of the journey."

The Great White Tiger chuckled gently. "No, my little ones. Now that you have learned to trust my love, we will have many great adventures ahead."

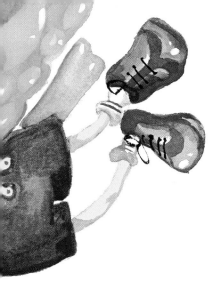

"We'll be there, too!"

Big Billy and his friends looked up to see Toodaloo, Lou, Lulu, and Bartholomew circle the carousel.

"And don't forget us!" cried Scooter and Raymond hopping out of the boat.

"How did *you* get here?" Miss Marbles giggled.

"We hitched a ride," Scooter replied with a grin.

"Shhh—what's that rustling sound??" Miss Marbles stopped to listen.

Everyone turned to face the woods.

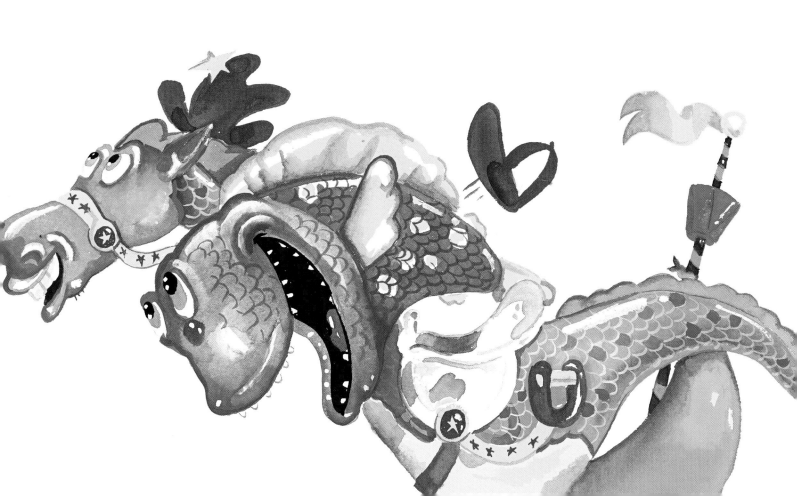

Creepshaw burst from the trees. "HEY! What about me??"

"Aaagghh!!" The animals all jumped back in fear.

"C-can I join your adventure?" Creepshaw stumbled in a squeaky voice.

The animals just looked at him, speechless.

"I'm really not a bad guy. I was just, I was in bad company, you know?" Creepshaw tried to explain as he approached the carousel. "I want to change. I want the Great White Tiger to love me like he does all of you. Old Reptillion doesn't even *like* me—even with all of my great ideas!"

"The Great White Tiger *already* loves you, Creepshaw," Big Billy said.

"Really??" Creepshaw tried to understand.

"Yes, really," Big Billy answered, smiling. "The whole point of this great adventure is letting the Great White Tiger love you and then, sharing his love with others."

"So, so you'll let me join the great adventure?"
Creepshaw asked, wiping a tear away.

"Of course!" the animals cried in unison.

Creepshaw smiled as the animals encircled him, cheering.

Big Billy gazed into the sky. "Great White Tiger, I have learned
that being loved by you is the adventure of a lifetime!"

The friends looked toward the sky and cried out
together, "It's the greatest adventure of all!"

The adventure of a lifetime is being loved by you.

When we're sad or when we're happy, we are loved by you.

When we feel alone, you're always there.

When friends are gone, you're there to care.

The great adventure of my lifetime is being loved by you.